THIS ONE'S FOR YOU!

Written and Photographed by

Zach Dillon

LANDMARK EDITIONS, INC.

P.O. Box 270169 • 1402 Kansas Avenue • Kansas City, Missouri 64127
(816) 241-4919

Dedicated to:
My family for their
love and encouragement,
and in memory of my grandmother.

I would like to thank the many individuals
who made my book possible:
My parents, Emily and Bill Dillon;
my English teachers, Debby Benzinger,
Jack Black, and Paula Fraser;
Josh Joslin and Sylvia Berry,
who helped stage the scenes;
and all the people who
worked as models for my book,
especially Nate Joslin, the model for Joey.

COPYRIGHT © 1999 BY ZACH DILLON

International Standard Book Number: 0-933849-72-9 (LIB.BDG.)

Library of Congress Cataloging-in-Publication Data
Dillon, Zach, 1985-
    This one's for you! / written and photographed by Zach Dillon.
    p. cm.
    Summary: After the death of his mother, Joey resents his father, who
has made the difficult decision of having her life-support systems turned
off and who has always been too busy to pay attention to him.
    ISBN 0-933849-72-9 (lib.bdg. : alk. paper)
    [1. Death—Fiction.   2. Grief—Fiction.
    3. Fathers and sons—Fiction.]

    I. Title.
    PZ7.D57975Th   1999
    [Fic]—dc21   99-19126
                                                      CIP

Creative Coordinator: David Melton
Editorial Coordinator: Nancy R. Thatch
Computer Graphics Coordinator: Brian Hubbard

Printed in the United States of America

Landmark Editions, Inc.
P.O. Box 270169
1402 Kansas Avenue
Kansas City, Missouri 64127
(816) 241-4919

Visit our Website — www.LandmarkEditions.com

The 1998 Panel of Judges

Richard F. Abrahamson, Ph.D.
    Director of Graduate Programs in
    Literature for Children and Adolescents
    University of Houston, TX

Kaye Anderson, Ph.D.
    Associate Professor, Teacher Education
    California State University at Long Beach

Barbara Diment, Library Media Specialist
    Portland Jewish Academy, Portland, OR

Jane Y. Ferguson, Editor
    CURRICULUM ADMINISTRATOR

Dorothy Francis, Instructor
    Institute of Children's Literature
    Author — METAL DETECTING FOR TREASURE

Patricia B. Henry, Teacher
    Wyoming State Reading Council Coordinator

Brian Hubbard, Associate Editor
    Landmark Editions, Inc.

Joyce E. Juntune, Lecturer
    Department of Education, Psychology
    Texas A & M University

Beverly Kelley, Library Media Specialist
    Linden West Elementary School, North Kansas City, MO

Lucinda Kennaley, Home Educator
    Kansas City, MO

Jean Kern, Library Media Specialist
    Educational Consultant, Landmark Editions, Inc.

Joyce Leibold, Teacher
    Educational Consultant, Landmark Editions, Inc.

Eathel McNabb, Teacher
    Educational Consultant, Landmark Editions, Inc.

Teresa M. Melton, Associate Editor
    and Contest Director, Landmark Editions, Inc.

John Micklos, Jr., Editor
    READING TODAY
    International Reading Association

Helen Redmond, Teacher of the Gifted
    Indian Woods Middle School, Overland Park, KS

Shirley Ross, Librarian, President Emeritus
    Missouri Association of School Librarians

Philip Sadler, Professor Emeritus, Children's Literature
    Director, Annual Children's Literature Festival
    Central Missouri State University

Cathy R. Salter, Writer and Educational Consultant
    The National Geographic Society

N.A Stonecipher, School Counselor & Psychologist
    T.J. Melton Elementary School, Grove, OK

Bonnie L. Swade, Teacher of English & Speech, Grade 9
    Pioneer Trail Junior High School, Olathe, KS

Nan Thatch, Editorial Coordinator
    Landmark Editions, Inc.

Barbara Upson, Youth Services Specialist
    Corinth Library, Prairie Village, KS

Kate Waters, Senior Editor
    Scholastic Hardcover Books
    Author — ON THE MAYFLOWER

Teresa L. Weaver, Library Media Specialist
    League City Intermediate School, League City, TX

Authors:

Carol S. Adler — MORE THAN A HORSE
Sandy Asher — WHERE DO YOU GET YOUR IDEAS?
Dana Brookins — ALONE IN WOLF HOLLOW
Clyde Robert Bulla — THE CHALK BOX KID
Scott Corbett — THE LEMONADE TRICK
Julia Cunningham — DORP DEAD
David Harrison — THE PURCHASE OF SMALL SECRETS
Carol Kendall — THE GAMMAGE CUP
Colleen O'Shaughnesy McKenna — GOOD GRIEF...THIRD GRADE!
Barbara Robinson — THE WORST BEST SCHOOL YEAR EVER
Ivy Ruckman — IN CARE OF CASSIE TUCKER
Theodore Taylor — THE HOSTAGE
Elvira Woodruff — THE ORPHAN OF ELLIS ISLAND

Authors and Illustrators:

Drew Carson — SUMMER DISCOVERY
Elizabeth Haidle — ELMER THE GRUMP
Laura Hughes — BRIGHT EYES AND THE BUFFALO HUNT
Amy Jones — ABRACADABRA
Jonathan Kahn — PATULOUS, THE PRAIRIE RATTLESNAKE
Benjamin Kendall — ALIEN INVASIONS
Gillian McHale — DON'T BUG ME!
David Melton — WRITTEN & ILLUSTRATED BY...
Jayna Miller — TOO MUCH TRICK OR TREAT
Kristin Pedersen — THE SHADOW SHOP
Lauren Peters — PROBLEMS AT THE NORTH POLE
Justin Rigamonti — THE PIGS WENT MARCHING OUT!
Anna Riphahn — THE TIMEKEEPER
Steven Shepard — FOGBOUND
Erica Sherman — THE MISTS OF EDEN —
                NATURE'S LAST PARADISE

THIS ONE'S FOR YOU!

When we began THE NATIONAL WRITTEN & ILLUSTRATED BY...AWARDS CONTEST FOR STUDENTS, I predicted that the books created by students would be more than just cutesy kids' books. My prediction has been proven correct. While many of the winning books are fun and entertaining, a number of them also deal with important and sensitive subjects, namely: *Broken Arrow Boy; Life in the Ghetto; Who Owns the Sun?; A Stone Promise; and The Mists of Eden.*

THIS ONE'S FOR YOU!, written by thirteen-year-old Zach Dillon, offers a *tour de force* of human emotions. When Zach's grandmother died, he discovered the pain of grief, and he began to wonder how a child would be affected by the death of a parent. So he decided to write about a fictional character named Joey and tell what happened to the boy after his mother died.

As a writer, Zach entered Joey's mind and explored the emotions the boy experienced. He traveled into the heart of Joey's pain and sorrow, lived the boy's feelings, and created this exceptional story.

THIS ONE'S FOR YOU! is not an easy book to read because the emotions of grief are not easy ones to experience. But all books are not supposed to be easy nor lighthearted. This is a serious book about a serious subject.

I am pleased that the illustrations are photographs, because I think it is good for young readers to have the opportunity to see sequential photographic illustrations, which are used rarely in juvenile or adult books today. The creation of illustrative photographs is an art form that requires the same exacting thought and preparation that drawn or painted pictures need. The photographic artist must select the models, find the locations, and compose the scenes that will add to the information and the moods presented in the narrative.

Zach is an interesting young man with whom to work. He is very quick to get ideas, and he writes with the speed of summer lightning — *quick! quick! quick! fast! fast! fast!* Nevertheless, the scenes in Zach's book are wonderful to read because they are beautifully composed and structured. All of them have good beginnings, middles, and ends. Each scene by itself is well rounded and complete and, just as importantly, each one moves the narrative forward to the next scene, which is exactly what it should do.

THIS ONE'S FOR YOU! is an extraordinary experience, one that is sure to touch the heart and mind of anyone who has the privilege to read it. I now invite you to begin that experience for yourself.

— David Melton
Creative Coordinator
Landmark Editions, Inc

Joey turns on the TV.

Bear wants some attention.

Joey loves to play basketball.

"No, Bear! Don't go in the street!"

"I'll get the ball."

Everyone who watched the five o'clock news that evening knew about the terrible wreck on Highway 67. Four cars and a semi-trailer truck were involved in the accident. Three people had been killed. Two others were in critical condition.

When Joey got home from school that afternoon, he turned on the television, but he didn't watch it. If he had, he might have seen his mother's car. But he probably wouldn't have recognized it because it was so twisted and crushed.

Joey's attention instead was on Bear, his Labrador retriever. Bear was barking and running back and forth, which was his way of saying he was ready to play one-on-one.

Joey glanced at the TV picture of an ambulance racing toward the hospital, then turned off the set. He grabbed his basketball, and he and Bear ran outside to the backyard. Bear barked with excitement as Joey dribbled the ball across the driveway and tossed it through the hoop.

Joey loved to play basketball. He had made the team at school, and he was one of the best players. This year the school had the strongest team ever. Halfway through the season, they still were undefeated. Joey's mother had come to every game. His father had never found the time to attend even one of them.

Joey aimed and shot the ball again. *Swish!* It went into the hoop and dropped to the pavement below. Before he could get the ball, Bear ran after it. He hit the ball with his front paws, knocking it across the driveway and into the street.

When the dog chased after the ball, Joey yelled, "No, Bear! Don't go in the street!"

Just as a car passed in front of him, Bear stopped

Joey's father comes home.

"Which hospital is she in?"

"Is Mom badly hurt?"   "I don't know."

obediently at the curb and waited for Joey to get the ball.

"Don't ever go into the street!" Joey scolded as he walked back to the driveway.

Bear barked, then jumped up and knocked the ball out of Joey's hands. To Bear's delight, the game was on again!

When Joey's father drove his station wagon into the driveway, Joey and Bear backed out of the way. Noticing his wife's car was not there, his father asked, "Where's your mother?"

"I don't know," answered Joey.

"Well, she should have been home by now," his father said. "Did she leave a note?"

"I didn't see one," Joey replied. "Say, Dad, do you remember that I have a game tomorrow?"

"Gosh, Joey," his father told him, "I wish I could be there, but I've got to work."

"So what's new?" Joey said, shrugging his shoulders.

"I'm sorry," his father apologized. "Maybe next time."

As they walked into the house, the telephone rang.

"That's probably your mother now," Joey's father said.

He took the phone from the receiver and answered, "Hello. Yes, this is John Mason. Yes, Ellen Mason is my wife. What? When did it happen? Is she all right? Which hospital is she in? I'll be right there.

"Come with me, Joey," he said, hanging up the phone. "Your mother has been in an accident, and she's in the hospital."

Joey and his father ran to the car and got inside. His father started the engine and backed the car into the street.

"Is Mom badly hurt?" asked Joey.

"I don't know," his father replied. "She was in a car wreck. That's all I was told."

They rush to the Emergency Room.

"I'll tell the doctor you're here."

Joey's father has to fill out the forms.

The doctor talks to Joey's father.

When they got to the hospital, Joey and his father rushed to the Emergency Room entrance. They hurried inside and walked to the reception desk.

"I'm John Mason," his father said to the woman who was standing there. "Someone called me and said my wife, Ellen Mason, was in the emergency room."

The woman looked at him and replied, "Yes, she is. I'll tell the doctor you're here. While you're waiting, you need to fill out these," she said, handing Joey's father some information forms.

Joey followed his father to the corner of the room and sat down beside him. While his father completed the forms, Joey waited. He saw other people come into the room and talk to the receptionist. Some of them seemed very worried and upset. One woman started crying.

When the doctor finally came to the door, Joey's father stood up. "Wait here, Joey," he said. Then he went over to the doctor.

Joey watched while the two men talked. After a few minutes, the doctor left, and Joey's father walked back to him.

"They're taking your mother into surgery now," his father told him.

"She's going to be all right, isn't she?" Joey asked him anxiously.

"They're doing all they can," his father replied.

They both sat and waited. His father read the evening newspaper and looked repeatedly at his watch. For a while, Joey looked through some magazines.

Then he got up and went over to watch some tropical fish that were in a tank by the wall. As he got closer, his magnified face in the glass startled the fish, and they scurried into their hiding places. That made Joey laugh, and for a few minutes, he made faces at them. But he soon became bored with this, and he stopped. He was glad he had gotten a dog instead of fish. Dogs are a lot more fun, he thought.

"There's a snack bar downstairs," his father told him. "Are you getting hungry?"

Joey looks at the tropical fish.

Two ham sandwiches, a bag of chips, and a Coke.

"Mom wouldn't approve of this food."

Other people are in the waiting room, too.

"I'm starved," replied Joey.

Two ham sandwiches, a bag of potato chips, and a Coke took care of his hunger.

"Mom wouldn't approve of this kind of food for dinner," Joey said.

"Then, we won't tell her," his father replied, winking at Joey and smiling.

When Joey and his father returned to the waiting room, the receptionist told them to go to the intensive care unit on the fourth floor. Once there, they were shown to another waiting room.

Joey noticed a man and woman who sat at the other end of the room. It looked as if they had been there a long time. Empty coffee cups and a tray of half-eaten food cluttered the floor at their feet. The woman looked very tired. She was leaning her head on the man's shoulder. Joey wondered if her mother was in intensive care, too.

There was a TV in the room. Joey turned it on and tried all the channels. The most interesting program

he found was a game show, so he watched that. He attempted to answer all the questions, but he was tired and had trouble concentrating. He kept worrying about his mother. Finally, he leaned his head back against the chair and went to sleep.

Joey didn't know how long he slept — one hour, or maybe two — when he heard someone call his father's name. He watched his father step into the hallway and talk to a doctor. After the doctor left, Joey's father stood silently in the doorway for some time.

Joey finally got up and went to him. "How's Mom?" he asked.

"She's out of surgery and in the recovery room," his father replied, trying not to look so worried.

"Can we see her?" asked Joey.

"Not yet."

They returned to their chairs and sat down. Joey was soon asleep again.

Joey is surprised to see Aunt Harriet.

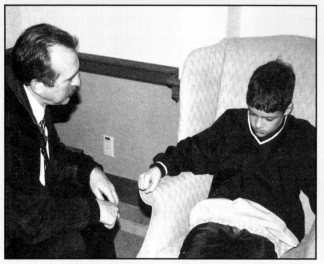
"I can take you in to see your mother now."

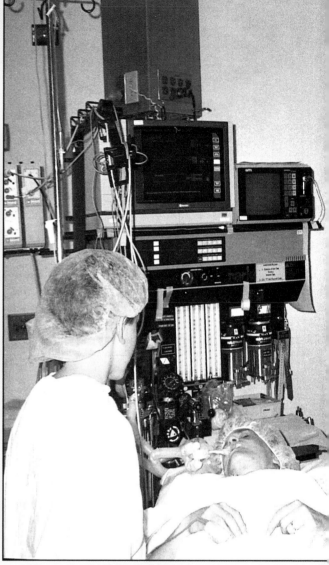
The nurse opens the curtain.

When Joey woke up, it was morning. He was quite surprised to see Aunt Harriet was there.

"Aunt Harriet is going to take you home and fix you some breakfast," his father told him.

"Aren't you coming with us?" Joey asked.

"No," his father replied. "I have to stay here for a while longer."

Although he didn't want to, Joey went with her.

Aunt Harriet wasn't really his aunt. She was his mother's aunt. This made her Joey's great-aunt. She was sixty-four years old, but she was a lot of fun. Joey really liked Aunt Harriet, but it wasn't the same as having his mother there.

About noon the next day, Joey's father came home long enough to shower and put on clean clothing.

"Your mother is still asleep," he told Joey. "I'll call you just as soon as she wakes up."

In the evening his father phoned Aunt Harriet and asked her to bring Joey to the hospital. When they got off the elevator, they hurried to the intensive care waiting room. Joey's father met them there.

"I can take you in to see your mother now," he told Joey. "But I have to warn you that she was very badly injured, and she is in serious condition. They have a number of machines connected to her. These are life-support systems that keep her heart beating and her lungs breathing. Her face is badly bruised, and she still is in a coma."

"What's that?" Joey wondered.

"A state of deep sleep," his father answered.

"Can she hear me?"

"I'm not sure," his father said, "but it's important that you talk to her as if she can."

Joey took a deep breath. "Okay," he said, and he followed his father into the intensive care unit.

When the nurse opened the curtain that separated

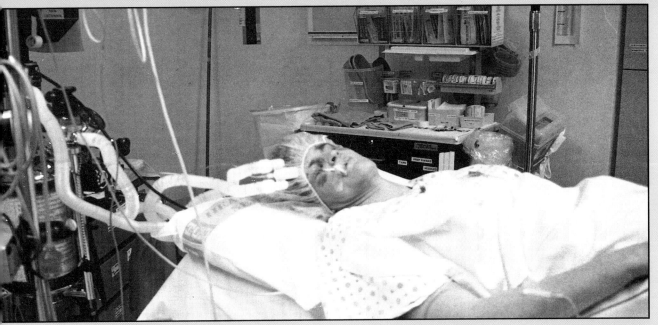
Joey's mother's face is terribly bruised and swollen.

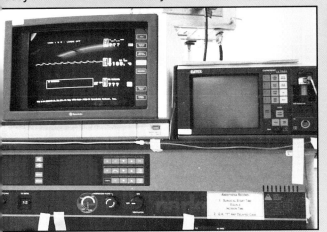
The machines make beeping noises.

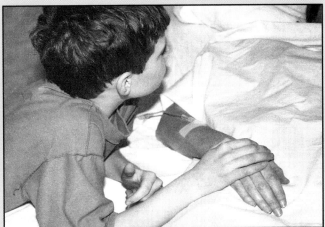
"Hi, Mom. It's me — Joey."

his mother's bed from the other patients, Joey stopped abruptly. At first he wasn't sure the person in the bed was his mother. Her face *was* terribly bruised and so swollen. There were tubes in her mouth, in her nose, and attached to her arms. Behind her bed, machines were making beeping noises.

"Are you all right, Joey?" his father asked.

Joey nodded his head and stepped closer to his mother's side.

"Hi, Mom. It's me — Joey," he said softly.

He hoped she would open her eyes and smile, but she didn't move.

"I'm sorry you were hurt, Mom, but you're going to get better real soon. You'll be home before you know it, and you'll be coming to my basketball games — just like you always did."

His mother offered no response.

"Mom, the team's playing again next week," he said. "Like I always do, I'll make a basket just for you."

Then Joey reached out and gently touched his mother's hand.

"I'll see you soon, Mom," he said.

When Joey stepped out of the room, Aunt Harriet went in to see his mother for a few minutes. Although Joey wanted to stay at the hospital, his father insisted that he go home with Aunt Harriet.

"Someone has to take care of Bear," his father said.

At home Joey watched TV for a while, but he couldn't concentrate on it for very long. His thoughts kept returning to his mother.

Sometimes Bear was a distraction. He would run into the kitchen and bump into Aunt Harriet's legs, which always made her let out a sharp little squeal. Then she would scold Bear and call to Joey, "Get your dog out of the kitchen!"

Aunt Harriet definitely was not a "dog person."

Joey's friend, Brendan, stops by.

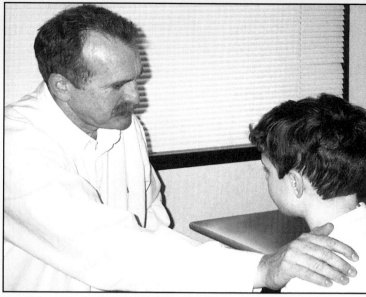

"I'm sorry to have to tell you this," says Joey's father.

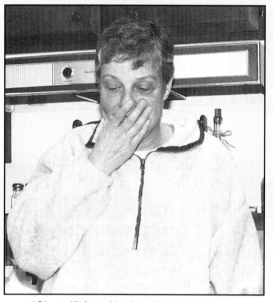

"Oh, no!" Aunt Harriet cries.

Joey rushes to his room.

That afternoon Joey's friend, Brendan, came by the house after school.

"Hi, Joey. I'm sorry about your mom," he said.

"Thanks," Joey replied. Then, not wanting to talk about it, he changed the subject. "Have I missed much at school?" he asked.

"Not much," said Brendan with a smile. "But you did miss something funny in science class today. When Mr. Kert opened the box of frogs for us to dissect, the frogs were still alive. The company must have sent the wrong order.

"Anyway, the frogs jumped out of the box and started hopping around the room. We had to catch all of them," laughed Brendan. "It was really wild."

"It sure sounds like it," said Joey, and he laughed halfheartedly.

"Well," said Brendan, looking at his watch, "I'd better get home for dinner. I just thought I'd come over and say hi."

"I'm glad you did," Joey told him. "I'll be seeing you."

"Right," Brendan replied. "I hope your mother gets better soon," he said and left.

About nine o'clock that night, Bear ran to the kitchen and barked. Then Joey heard his father's car pull into the driveway and stop, but his father didn't come in for some time. When Joey started to go outside, Aunt Harriet stopped him and suggested that he wait. Finally, they heard the car door shut, and his father opened the back door and stepped inside the house.

"How's Mom?" Joey asked quickly.

His father sat down and placed his hand on his son's shoulder. "Joey," he said, "I'm so sorry to have

The funeral is three days later.

Joey sits between Aunt Harriet and his father.

Joey's favorite picture.

Joey and his father hold roses.

Joey hears all he can stand.

to tell you this. Your mother died about an hour ago."

"Oh, no!" Aunt Harriet exclaimed, and she started crying.

Joey couldn't hold back his tears either. He pulled away from his father and ran to his room. Bear followed close behind.

The funeral was held three days later. The church was filled with beautiful flowers, and many relatives and friends attended. During the service, the minister told what a wonderful wife and parent Joey's mother had been.

Joey sat between Aunt Harriet and his father. He tried to listen, but his mind kept drifting. The sounds he heard were like distant voices in a hollow tunnel.

After the service was over, Joey reached into his pocket and pulled out his favorite photograph — the one of he and his mother, and Bear — and he quietly placed the picture in the casket.

"Goodbye, Mom," he said softly. "I love you."

At the cemetery, the minister said another prayer. Then Joey and his father each laid a rose on the casket.

Afterwards, many people came to their house. There was more food than they could eat. Everyone talked about Joey's mother. Some spoke of fond memories of her. Others told humorous stories about what his mother had said or done. There was even a lot of laughter. This surprised Joey. He didn't think anything was funny.

After a while, he had heard all he could stand. He went to his room, but even there, he couldn't stop thinking about his mother and how much he missed her.

The day Joey had dreaded finally arrives.

The bus ride to school.

When he sees Sarah walking toward him, Joey turns away.

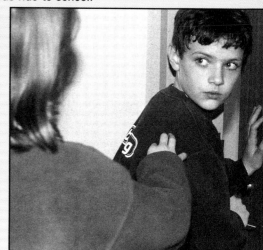
He makes a quick escape.

Joey dreaded the first day he had to go back to school. He knew everyone had heard about his mother's death. He knew his friends would feel sorry for him. He just didn't want them to tell him how sorry they felt. Their feeling sorry without saying it would be enough, he thought.

But Joey knew all his classmates wouldn't leave it there. Some were bound to say something. He just hoped when they did, they would be quick and get it over with.

Most of all, Joey didn't want to cry in front of anyone. Somehow he would have to keep himself together.

When he got on the school bus that morning, he felt like everyone was staring at him. As he made his way down the aisle, a few students said, "Hi, Joey."

A couple of them glanced up at him, then quickly looked away as if they didn't know what to do. Joey didn't know what to do either. So he sat down in the first empty seat he came to and just stared straight ahead.

Ralph Mueller, the boy who was seated across the aisle from him, said, "How ya doin', Joey?"

"Fine," Joey answered.
Ralph didn't say any more. Joey was grateful for that.

When Joey entered the main hall of the school building, he saw Sarah Wilson walking toward him. Sarah was definitely the last person Joey wanted to talk to because she was such a gossip. He knew that whatever he said to her might as well be published in the school paper or announced at the school assembly.

Just before Sarah reached him, Joey turned and rushed into the one place the girl couldn't follow him — the boy's rest room. He knew he wouldn't be able to avoid Sarah for the rest of the school year. "But not today," he said to himself. "Not today."

After the bell rang and the halls had cleared, Joey stepped out of the rest room and hurried to class.

That afternoon, while his history teacher, Ms. Pennock, was reading to the students about the Battle of Bunker Hill, Joey's mind kept wandering. He could not stop thinking about his mother. He remembered

Joey's mind keeps wandering.

"Joey!" Ms. Pennock says, "Please stay after class."

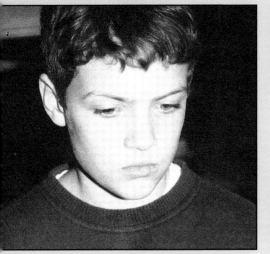
"Do you want to see me?" Joey asks.

"You don't have to explain," his teacher tells him.

the day she had helped him put up the basketball hoop and how she had made lemonade afterwards.

He and his mother had laughed about something that was so funny, they couldn't stop laughing. That made Bear bark and run back and forth in the kitchen. What had they laughed about? Joey wondered. He couldn't remember.

When he heard Ms. Pennock call out his name, he realized he had been daydreaming. He looked blankly at his teacher.

"Will you please stay after class?" Ms. Pennock asked him.

"Yes, Ma'am," Joey replied.

"Oh, boy!" he thought to himself. "Now I'm in really big trouble!"

Ms. Pennock was known as the strictest teacher in school. She was very stern most of time, and she rarely smiled. No one liked her. Some students were even afraid of her.

After the bell rang and all the others had left the classroom, Joey walked to Ms. Pennock's desk.

"Did you want to see me?" he asked quietly.

"Yes, I do," Ms. Pennock replied. "I noticed that you had trouble paying attention in class today."

"I was..." Joey started to say.

"You don't have to explain," Ms. Pennock said. "I understand what you're going through. My mother died last spring. For a long time, it was very difficult for me to come to school and keep my mind on what I was doing. But I kept trying and, although you may not think so now, it will get easier. I just want you to know that if you have trouble paying attention, I will certainly understand."

"I'll remember that," said Joey. "May I go now?"

"Of course," she answered. Then Ms. Pennock actually smiled. Joey noticed that it was a nice smile.

As Joey walked to the school bus, he recalled that last winter he had seen Ms. Pennock with her mother at the shopping mall. He hadn't known that her mother had died since then.

Maybe most students thought Ms. Pennock was mean, but Joey knew he never would think that again.

Joey is hardly able to believe what he hears.

When Joey got home from school that afternoon, Aunt Harriet was busy talking on the telephone with one of her friends. She didn't hear Joey come into the house.

"Poor Joey," he overheard her say, "losing his mother at such a young age. It was an awful experience for his father, too. It was so difficult for John to have to make the decision to let the doctors disconnect the life-support systems from Ellen."

"What?" Joey gasped, hardly able to believe what he had heard — *disconnect the life-support systems!* His father had let his mother die! How could he have done such a horrible thing?

Joey grabbed his basketball and ran to the backyard. Bear ran after him, ready to play, but Joey was in no mood for playing. He wanted to start screaming. He just stood there instead and kept throwing the ball against the side of the house.

When his father came home, Joey was in the driveway, waiting for him.

"Did you tell the doctors they could take my mother off the life-support systems?" he demanded to know.

"Who told you that?" his father asked.

Aunt Harriet stepped outside. "I'm afraid he heard me on the telephone," she said. "I'm sorry. I didn't know he was home."

"Did you tell them to let my mother die?" Joey persisted.

"I had to," his father replied as calmly as he could. "Your mother had a terrible head injury. The doctors told me her brain was dead and it was impossible for them to revive her. The only thing the support systems did was keep her heart beating and her lungs breathing. Joey, I did what your mother would have wanted."

"Without even asking *me* what *I* wanted?" Joey snapped back.

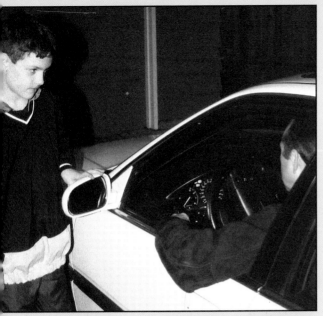

When his father comes home, Joey is waiting.

"Did you tell them to let my mother die?"

"I want you to know, I will *never* forgive you!"

"I couldn't ask you."

"Why not?" Joey pressed.

"It wasn't a decision you should have been asked to make," his father replied.

"Mom wouldn't have done that to you!" Joey said.

"You're wrong, Joey. Your mother would have done the same for me. It had to be done."

"You still should have asked *me* what *I* thought!" Joey insisted.

"No, Joey, I shouldn't have asked you," his father replied. "You're a child. You should not be asked to make that kind of decision. It was an adult decision, and I had to make it by myself."

Joey clenched his teeth and said, "I want you to know that I will *never* forgive you!"

Then Joey turned away and ran into the house. Bear followed close at his heels.

"I am so sorry, John," Aunt Harriet said.

"It's not your fault," he told her gently. "Joey had to know some time."

During the next week, Joey avoided his father as much as he could. When his father came into a room, Joey would leave the room. If his father asked him a question, Joey would give him the shortest possible answer.

Since his father left for work early every morning, Joey didn't have to face him at breakfast. He was thankful for that.

But at night, his father always got home in time for dinner. Joey had to eat with him and Aunt Harriet, though he always let them do most of the talking. Joey would eat as quickly as he could, then excuse himself from the table.

15

At the basketball game.

Joey can't help but think of his mother.

His father and Aunt Harriet are there.

Joey doesn't want to hear their praises.

Joey didn't mention his next basketball game to his father. Instead, he rode to the gym with Brendan and his parents.

Joey kept thinking about his mother not being there. During every game he had played, he always would look at her at least once and nod his head. That was their "special signal." She knew he was telling her, "This one's for you, Mom," and she would watch him sink the ball into the basket. Joey wouldn't be able to do that tonight.

Aunt Harriet came to the game. That pleased Joey. Even so, he didn't tell her about the "special signal." He wasn't ready to share that with anyone.

The game went well, with Joey's team taking an early lead. At the end of the first quarter, Joey got the ball. As he dribbled it down the court, he happened to glance up into the stands. What he saw made him lose his concentration. His father was sitting next to Aunt Harriet!

Joey stumbled and fell forward. He dropped the ball, and it was grabbed by the opposing guard. Joey got up quickly, but it took him some time to get his mind back into the game. He had always been an aggressive player. Now, the anger he was feeling toward his father drove him to play even harder. That afternoon his team won easily.

At dinner that evening, Aunt Harriet and his father kept talking about the game and how well Joey had done.

"You played a great game, Joey," his father said.

"I was okay," he replied. "You just never saw me play before."

"I'm trying to correct that now," his father said.

"You don't need to bother," Joey told him. "I don't

Aunt Harriet goes home.

Joey doesn't want to talk to his father at dinner.

Joey is surprised to see his father at the next game, too.

It isn't his father he wants to see.

want my basketball games to interfere with your work."

Then he stood up abruptly, excused himself, and went to his room to do homework.

That weekend Aunt Harriet went home. Joey told her he would miss her. She said she would miss him, too, and she even remarked that she would miss Bear. They both laughed at that. To Joey's surprise, his aunt patted Bear on the head before she left.

Joey dreaded having dinner alone with his father that night. He brought a book to the table with him and said he had so much homework, he needed to read while he ate.

"Fine," his father replied, and he took some papers out of his briefcase and started reading, too. In the quiet room, Bear stretched out on the floor and fell asleep.

The homework excuse worked, so Joey kept using it every night. His father also seemed to have plenty to read, so it didn't become a problem.

Joey didn't expect to see his father at the next basketball game, but to his surprise, his father was there. He sat in the stands and cheered his son all the way.

His father was at the next game, too. And the next. Each time he came to a game, it annoyed Joey even more because it wasn't his father he wanted to see in the stands — it was his mother.

Joey wanted to nod his head and give his mother their "special signal." Just once more, he longed to say, "This one's for you, Mom." Joey knew he would never say those words to his father, no matter how many games his dad attended.

"It's me," the voice replied cheerfully. "I'm home."

"Hi, Bear. Where's Joey?" she asks.

R-i-n-n-n-n-n-g !

Something else unexpected happened one morning. Joey and Bear were alone in the house. They were in the living room where Joey was watching TV. Bear suddenly raised his head and barked. Then he stood up and ran into the kitchen.

The back door opened and Joey heard a voice say, "Hi, Bear. Where's Joey?"

"Who is it?" Joey called out.

"It's me," the voice replied cheerfully. "I'm home." Joey recognized the voice.

"Mom!" he exclaimed, and he jumped up and ran to the kitchen. When he saw his mother, Joey rushed to her and threw himself into her arms.

"Oh, Mom!" he cried. "I'm so glad you're home. I missed you so much!"

"I've missed you, too," she laughed, "and I've missed Bear."

"Where have you been?" Joey asked.

"Not far away," his mother replied with a smile.

"But the doctors said you were dead!"

"Well, they were mistaken," she told him. "They just *thought* I had died."

"Dad thought you were dead, too," Joey insisted.

"Oh, that's just what they told him, but it wasn't true," she explained. "Now I'm back and everything is like it used to be."

"Oh, Mom, I'm so happy you're home!"

"So am I," his mother laughed, and then she petted Bear and hugged Joey again.

R-i-n-n-n-n-n-g !

The shrill sound of the alarm clock was piercing to Joey's ears! He sat up in bed and looked about the room.

"Mom!" he called out. "Where are you?"

There was no answer.

Then Joey realized that his mother had not come home. It had only been a dream — a beautiful dream — a wonderful dream — an awful dream!

Joey finally reached over and turned off the alarm. He could not hold back his tears. He cried until he could cry no more.

"Surprise!" his father says, "We're going camping."

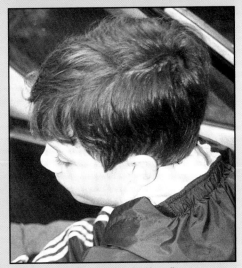

"I don't want to do that."

But Joey helps load the car anyway.

Before they reach the highway, it starts to rain.

One Friday afternoon, when Joey came home from school, his father's station wagon was in the driveway. The hatch was up, and camping gear lay in piles nearby. Joey walked over to the station wagon and stood there, looking puzzled.

"Surprise!" his father said as he carried a bedroll from the garage.

"What's going on?" Joey asked.

"We're going camping up at Blue Lake. You and I are going to spend some time together and do some fishing. Pack your clothes and help me get all of this stuff into the car."

"But I've made plans," Joey protested. "I'm supposed to sleep over at Brendan's tonight."

"Then call Brendan and tell him you can't," his father replied.

"But I don't want to do that," Joey said defiantly.

"It's not up for a vote," his father directed. "Do as I told you."

Joey knew his father meant it.

"Okay," he said as he stomped into the house to phone Brendan and give him the bad news. Then he piled some clothes into a duffel bag and carried it outside. He didn't say a word while he and his father loaded everything into the station wagon.

When Joey let Bear in the back seat, the dog barked with excitement. He loved to ride in the car. Bear liked Joey's father, too, and he raised up and gave him a friendly lick on the back of the neck.

"Traitor!" scolded Joey under his breath, and he gave Bear a disgusted look as he climbed into the back seat beside the dog.

"You can sit up front with me," his father offered.

"No thank you," Joey replied stubbornly.

"Suit yourself," his father said. Then he started the car and backed it out of the driveway.

Before they had reached the highway, it started to rain, not just a slow, easy rain, but a downpour. Joey sat back and watched torrents of raindrops splash against the window, and he thought about the lake.

This time the trip seems longer than ever before.

It continues to rain.

Everything outside looks gray and wet.

Bear seems to enjoy the ride, but Joey doesn't.

Blue Lake was one of his family's favorite camping places. Joey had gone there with his mother and father for the last four years. His mother had always made the three-hour car ride fun. She had been the one to invent games and think of songs to entertain the family during those trips.

Last year's camping trip had been the best one. They caught more fish than ever, and they went swimming every day. Bear liked that, too. He always hit the water like a cannonball and splashed everyone around.

"I'll bet the rain will stop by the time we get to the lake," his father said, trying to be cheerful.

He would lose that bet, because when they finally reached Blue Lake, it was raining so hard, they decided not to pitch their tent. They checked into a motel instead and spent the night.

It rained all day Saturday, too. Bear slept most of the day. Joey and his father watched TV in their motel room and ate their meals in silence at the restaurant.

Sunday morning it stopped raining for a few minutes, then started again. Shortly after lunch, Joey and his father packed their duffel bags and put them in the station wagon. Bear jumped into the car with them, and they headed for home.

"Well, we tried," his father sighed.

"It's not the same without Mom," Joey said flatly.

"Joey, it will never be the same," his father told him. "Our lives are different now. We have only each other. We have to make the best of that."

"Are you going to keep coming to the basketball

To pass the time, they watch TV.

They eat their meals in silence.

Joey's father finally gives up and they head for home.

"You miss her, too, don't you, Bear?"

games?" Joey inquired.

"Yes."

"You don't have to," Joey said quickly.

"I want to," his father replied.

"You never wanted to before," Joey snapped.

"Well, I want to be there now," his father said. "Sometimes we learn things as we go along in life, Joey. I'm trying to learn how to be a better parent. It hasn't been easy to learn how to do that, but I'm trying."

Joey folded his arms and tightened his lips. "You are not going to take my mother's place," he declared.

"I'm not trying to take her place," his father told him. "I don't want to be your mother. You had a wonderful mother. We both miss her. But she's gone and I'm here. I am your father, and I want to be your father. I

want you to think about that."

Joey mumbled his answer.

"What did you say?" his father asked.

"I said I will think about it."

"Good," his father said as he turned the station wagon onto the main highway.

In about three hours, they were home. After they unloaded the car and carried their duffel bags into the house, Joey's father stretched out on the couch. He wanted to watch the news, but he didn't for long because he fell asleep.

Joey went to his room and sat down on his bed. Bear jumped up and lay down beside him.

"You miss her, too, don't you, Bear?" said Joey, hugging his dog. "I know you do."

The trip Joey and Bear make is not a short one.

Everything seems so quiet and peaceful.

Joey and Bear finally come to the cemetery.

Joey lays his bicycle on the grass.

During the next week, Joey did think about what his father had told him, but he had trouble sorting out his feelings. He couldn't stop resenting what his father had let the doctors do to his mother.

On Saturday afternoon, while his father enjoyed watching a football game on TV, Joey and Bear went outside. Joey got his bicycle from the garage, climbed onto it, and started riding. Bear ran after him.

Their trip would not be a short one. Joey would have to ride for almost an hour, yet it was a trip he had to take. He had wanted to make it for some time, but until today, he had not been ready. Now he thought he would be able to.

After he and Bear entered the cemetery, they went up the winding road and stopped. Joey got off his bicycle and laid it down on the grass. Then he and Bear walked to the marker that lay at the head of a grave — Joey's mother's grave.

"Hi, Mom. It's me — Joey," he finally said. "Bear's here, too. We just came to talk to you.

"Everything is going okay at school. I thought you'd like to know that I got an *A* on my spelling test last week. That's a first for me.

"Our basketball team has won every game, and it looks like we may make it to the playoffs. I thought you might like to know that, too.

"And guess what? Dad has been coming to the games. I'll bet that surprises you. It sure surprised

"Hi, Mom. It's me — Joey," he says. "Bear is here, too."

"The trouble is, I can't forgive Dad."

Joey and Bear start for home.

me. He's come to every game since you...since the accident...you know what I mean.

"Everything's all right at home," said Joey. Then he paused for a moment and sat down on the grass.

"Well, that's not exactly true," he continued. "Everything's not all right. It's not good at all. In fact, everything is terrible between Dad and me. He's trying to do more things with me, but we just don't get along.

"He cooks dinner almost every night. You're probably glad to hear that we eat plenty of vegetables. And Dad's cooking is pretty good, but it's not as good as yours, of course.

"But you see...the trouble is...I can't forgive Dad for letting the doctors take you off the life-support systems.

And I don't know what to do about it."

Joey reached out his hand, and he stroked the grass on his mother's grave, just the way she used to touch his hair.

"We've got to go now," he said, taking a deep breath. "Bear and I have to get home before dinner. I love you, Mom. We miss you so much."

Then Joey and Bear stood up. As they walked down the hill, the world seemed unusually quiet and still, and Joey felt more peaceful and a little less lonely.

He got on his bicycle, and he and Bear hurried toward home. Joey knew the football game would be over by now and his father would be wondering where they had gone.

"Where have you been?" his father demands to know.

The basketball rolls into the street.

Before Joey can stop him, Bear bounds into the street.

When Joey arrived home, his father was outside, waiting for him in the driveway.

"Where have you been?" he demanded to know.

"I just went for a ride," Joey answered.

"The rule is," his father said sternly, "you always tell me *when* you are going and *where* you are going. Where were you?"

"Bear and I went to the cemetery to visit Mom's grave."

"I see," his father said less sternly. "But you should have told me. I was worried about you."

"I'll tell you from now on," replied Joey.

His father looked at him for a few moments, then turned and walked slowly into the house. Joey followed him inside, got his basketball, and returned to the backyard.

He dribbled the ball across the driveway and shot it through the hoop. When the ball bounced on the pavement, Bear got to it first and hit the ball with his nose.

That made Joey laugh, and he ran for the ball. But Bear beat him to it again. The dog swatted the ball with his front paws and sent it rolling across the driveway and into the street.

Bear was so excited that he chased after the ball. Before Joey could stop him, Bear had bounded out into the street in front of an oncoming car.

"Bear!" screamed Joey.

The driver of the car slammed on the brakes, but it was too late. The car hit Bear with a resounding thud and knocked him to the other side of the street.

Hearing his son's scream and the screech of tires, Joey's father rushed out of the house. He ran across the street to where Joey was on his knees, trying to get Bear to move.

"It's not my fault!" the driver said excitedly as he hurried over to them. "Your dog ran in front of my car! Is he all right?"

Joey kneels down beside Bear.

Joey's father quickly lifts the large dog.

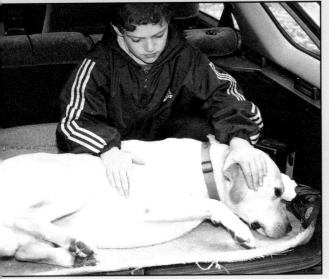
Joey climbs in beside Bear.

They rush to the veterinary hospital.

"We've got to get him to the vet," Joey's father said quickly. He lifted the large dog in his arms and carried him to the station wagon. Then he gently laid him down in the back.

Joey climbed in beside Bear and patted the dog's head. When Bear moaned, Joey tried to reassure him. "It's okay, Bear," he said. "You're going to be all right."

"I'm really sorry," the driver apologized.

"We don't blame you," Joey's father told him. Then he started the car and backed it out of the driveway.

"Someone help us!" cried Joey as he ran into the veterinary hospital. "My dog's been hit by a car!"

The vet's assistant quickly opened the door to the examination room. Joey's father carried Bear inside and laid him on the table.

Hearing all the commotion, Dr. Harrison hurried into the room.

"What's the matter?" she asked.

"My dog was hit by a car!" Joey told her excitedly.

Dr. Harrison started examining Bear. The room was silent, except for the dog's whimpering.

"He's going to be all right, isn't he?" Joey asked.

"We'll see," she replied quietly. "Let's roll this table into the next room so I can take some X-rays."

Joey and his father helped push the table down the hall.

"Bear is a very strong dog," Joey told Dr. Harrison.

"I'm sure he is," she said, "but he has received a terrible blow."

While Dr. Harrison and her assistant took X-rays, Joey and his father waited in the hallway.

"Bear knew he wasn't supposed to go into the street," Joey cried. "He wanted to get the ball so much that he just forgot."

"I know," his father said, trying to console him.

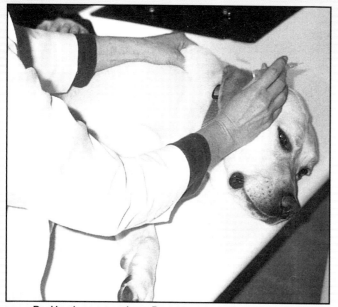
Dr. Harrison examines Bear.

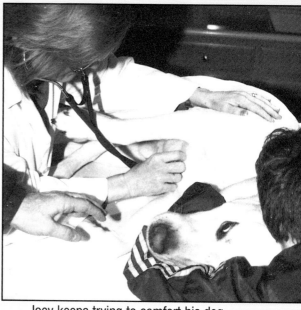
Joey keeps trying to comfort his dog.

"I'm afraid things don't look good," Dr. Harrison says.

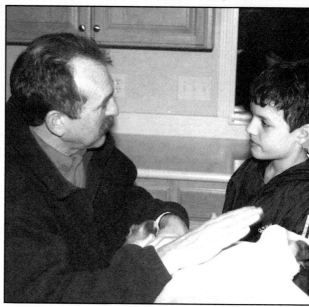
"What do you think we should do, Dad?" Joey asks.

When Dr. Harrison opened the door, Joey and his father hurried into the room. Joey stroked Bear's head and tried to comfort him. "It's okay, Bear," he said. "I'm here with you."

After studying the X-rays, Dr. Harrison took a deep breath and said, "I'm afraid things don't look good. Bear has a broken hip and a ruptured pelvis. There's a considerable amount of internal bleeding, too."

"But you can help him, can't you?" urged Joey.

"I don't know," replied Dr. Harrison. "You see, Joey, I could operate on Bear and put steel pins in his pelvis, and the bones might heal. But most likely, he would never be able to walk again because of the damage to his spinal cord.

"Even if Bear survives the operation," Dr. Harrison continued, "and I'm not sure he would, his liver or his kidneys may be so badly injured that he would die in a few days."

Joey was stunned. He didn't know what to say.

Then Joey's father spoke up. "Dr. Harrison, if Bear were your dog, what would you do?"

The veterinarian looked at Joey. "Bear is in a lot of pain," she said. "I would not want my dog to be in so much pain."

Joey turned to his father and asked, "What do you think we should do, Dad?"

"That's not a decision for me to make," his father replied. "Bear is your dog. You are the one who has to decide what to do."

"But, Dad, I love Bear," Joey tried to reason.

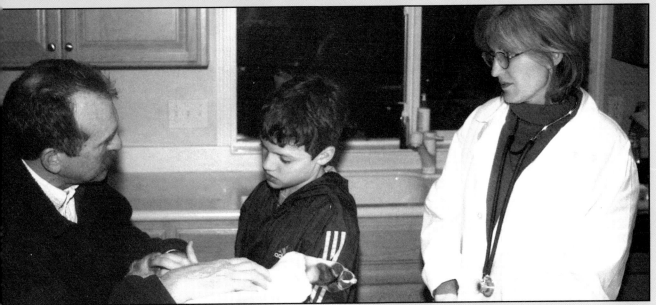

"Bear is your dog," his father tells him. "You are the one who has to decide what to do."

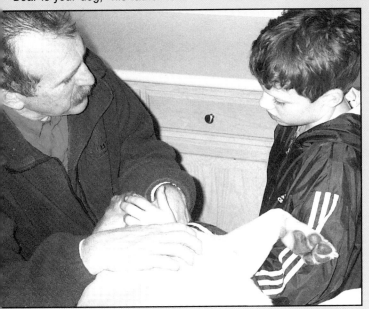

"But, I love Bear," Joey insists.

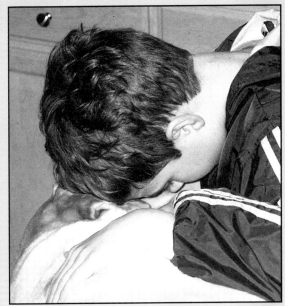

"I'm sorry, Bear," Joey says.

"I know you do," his father replied, "and because you love him so much, I'm sure you'll do what is best for him."

For a few moments, Joey looked thoughtfully at his father. Then he asked quietly, "Is that how you decided to let them remove the life-support systems from Mom?"

"Yes, Joey," his father said. "It was a decision I made with a lot of love."

Bear lay trembling on the examination table. When he started whimpering again, Joey wrapped his arms around his dog and gently laid his face against Bear's head.

"I'm sorry, Bear," he said, "but I can't let you be in so much pain."

Then Joey looked up at Dr. Harrison and asked, "It won't hurt him, will it?"

"No," she replied. "I'll just give him an injection, and Bear will drift peacefully into sleep."

"All right," Joey said, wiping the tears from his face. "Please stop Bear's pain."

Joey and his father stayed with Bear to the last. Joey stroked his dog's head and talked to him until Bear finally grew quiet and stopped breathing.

Joey hugged Bear one more time. Then he reached out and felt his father's comforting arms wrap around him.

Joey and his father had Bear's body cremated and his ashes sealed in an urn. Then, together, they buried the urn in a quiet corner of the backyard.

The stands are full today.

Joey's father cheers for the team.

The competition is fierce! The score is tied 56 to 56.

Both teams were playing their best.

"This one's for you, Dad."

... and the ball plunges through the hoop.

28

Joey's favorite picture of he and his dad.

For Joey and his father, it had been a season of painful losses — the loss of Joey's mother and the loss of Bear. It also had been a season of discovery for both of them — one that had brought better understanding and respect between them.

When Joey's basketball team made it to the playoffs, he and his father were really excited. They talked and laughed all the way while they were driving to the gym. When they arrived, Joey ran to the locker room to get ready for the game. His father hurried inside to take a seat in the stands.

That afternoon the competition on the basketball court was fierce! Neither team had been defeated all season. At halftime, the score was 26 to 26.

That afternoon Joey played better than he ever had before. His passes were sharp, his defense was tight, and his shooting was accurate. All of his teammates were playing their best, too, but so were their opponents.

At the end of the third quarter, the other team had pulled ahead four points — the score stood at 47 to 43. In the fourth quarter, Joey's team tied the score at 56 to 56.

With only forty seconds left in the game, the other team made two free throws to take a two-point lead. Then, with only nine seconds left, Brendan got the ball and passed it to Joey.

Joey caught the ball and charged forward, dribbling it across the court. He stopped just outside the three-point line. Then, pausing for only a moment, Joey looked up at his father and nodded his head at him.

"This one's for you, Dad," he said softly.

Then Joey took careful aim and released the ball. It arched high into the air and plunged downward through the center of the hoop.

Dav Pilkey
age 19

Lauren Peters
age 7

Benjamin Kendall
age 7

Amy Hagstrom
age 9

Michael Cain
age 11

Leslie A. MacKeen
age 9

Shintaro Maeda
age 8

A. Chandrasekhar
age 9

Dennis Vollmer
age 6

Alise Leggat
age 8

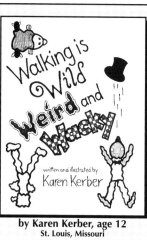

by Karen Kerber, age 12
St. Louis, Missouri
ISBN 0-933849-29-X   Full Color

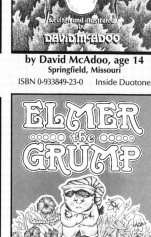

by David McAdoo, age 14
Springfield, Missouri
ISBN 0-933849-23-0   Inside Duotone

by Amy Hagstrom, age 9
Portola, California
ISBN 0-933849-15-X   Full Color

by Isaac Whitlatch, a
Casper, Wyoming
ISBN 0-933849-16-8   Full

WHO CAN FIX IT?

written & illustrated by
Leslie Ann MacKeen

by Leslie Ann MacKeen, age 9
Winston-Salem, North Carolina
ISBN 0-933849-19-2   Full Color

ELMER the GRUMP

- written & illustrated by -
ELIZABETH HAIDLE

by Elizabeth Haidle, age 13
Beaverton, Oregon
ISBN 0-933849-20-6   Full Color

Taddy McTinley and the Great Grey Grimly

written & illustrated by
Heidi Salter

by Heidi Salter, age 19
Berkeley, California
ISBN 0-933849-21-4   Full Color

Problem at the North Po

written & illustrated by
Lauren Peters

by Lauren Peters, a
Kansas City, Missouri
ISBN 0-933849-25-7   Full

OLIVER and the OIL SPILL

written and illustrated by
ARUNA CHANDRASEKHAR

by Aruna Chandrasekhar, age 9
Houston, Texas
ISBN 0-933849-33-8   Full Color

Life in the ghetto

written and illustrated by
ANIKA D. THOMAS

by Anika Thomas, age 13
Pittsburgh, Pennsylvania
ISBN 0-933849-34-6   Inside Two Colors

A STONE PROMISE
BY CARA REICHEL

by Cara Reichel, age 15
Rome, Georgia
ISBN 0-933849-35-4   Inside Two Colors

PATULO
THE PRAIRIE RATTLE

written and illustrated by
JONATHAN KAH

by Jonathan Kahn, a
Richmond Heights, Oh
ISBN 0-933849-36-2   Full

ALIEN INVASIONS

written and illustrated by
BENJAMIN KENDALL

by Benjamin Kendall, age 7
State College, Pennsylvania
ISBN 0-933849-42-7   Full Color

FOGBOUND

written and illustrated by
STEVEN SHEPARD

by Steven Shepard, age 13
Great Falls, Virginia
ISBN 0-933849-43-5   Full Color

CHANGES

written and illustrated by
TRAVIS WILLIAMS

by Travis Williams, age 16
Sardis, B.C., Canada
ISBN 0-933849-44-3   Inside Two Colors

A SPECIAL

written & illustrated by
DUBRAVKA KOLANOVIC

by Dubravka Kolanovic,
Savannah, Georgia
ISBN 0-933849-45-1   Full

Dav Pilkey, age 19
Cleveland, Ohio
0-933849-22-2   Full Color

by Dennis Vollmer, age 6
Grove, Oklahoma
ISBN 0-933849-12-5   Full Color

by Lisa Gross, age 12
Santa Fe, New Mexico
ISBN 0-933849-13-3   Full Color

by Stacy Chbosky, age 14
Pittsburgh, Pennsylvania
ISBN 0-933849-14-1   Full Color

Michael Cain, age 11
Annapolis, Maryland
0-933849-26-5   Full Color

by Amity Gaige, age 16
Reading, Pennsylvania
ISBN 0-933849-27-3   Full Color

by Adam Moore, age 9
Broken Arrow, Oklahoma
ISBN 0-933849-24-9   Inside Duotone

by Michael Aushenker, age 19
Ithaca, New York
ISBN 0-933849-28-1   Full Color

Jayna Miller, age 19
Zanesville, Ohio
0-933849-37-0   Full Color

by Bonnie-Alise Leggat, age 8
Culpepper, Virginia
ISBN 0-933849-39-7   Full Color

by Lisa Kirsten Butenhoff, age 13
Woodbury, Minnesota
ISBN 0-933849-40-0   Full Color

by Jennifer Brady, age 17
Columbia, Missouri
ISBN 0-933849-41-9   Full Color

Amy Jones, age 17
Shirley, Arkansas
0-933849-46-X   Full Color

by Shintaro Maeda, age 8
Wichita, Kansas
ISBN 0-933849-51-6   Full Color

by Miles MacGregor, age 12
Phoenix, Arizona
ISBN 0-933849-52-4   Full Color

by Kristin Pedersen, age 18
Etobicoke, Ont., Canada
ISBN 0-933849-53-2   Full Color

Travis Williams
age 16

Anika D. Thomas
age 13

Isaac Whitlatch
age 11

Elizabeth Haidle
age 13

Miles MacGregor
age 12

Jayna Miller
age 19

Jonathan Kahn
age 9

Stacy Chbosky
age 14

David McAdoo
age 12

Amity Gaige
age 16

Bright Eyes and the Buffalo Hunt
WRITTEN AND ILLUSTRATED BY Laura Hughes

by Laura Hughes, age 8
Woonsocket, Rhode Island
ISBN 0-933849-57-5   Full Color

CRITTER CRACKERS
THE ABC BOOK OF LIMERICKS
written and illustrated by KATHRYN BARRON

by Kathryn Barron, age 13
Emo, Ont., Canada
ISBN 0-933849-58-3   Full Color

Glory Trail
Written and Illustrated by Taramesha Maniatty

by Taramesha Maniatty, age 15
Morrisville, Vermont
ISBN 0-933849-59-1   Full Color

CIRCLE ADVENTURE
written and illustrated by LINDSEY WOL

by Lindsay Wolter, a
Cheshire, Connecticu
ISBN 0-933849-61-3   Full

THE TIMEKEEPER
Written & Illustrated by ANNA RIPHAHN

by Anna Riphahn, age 13
Topeka, Kansas
ISBN 0-933849-62-1   Full Color

DARIUS The Lonely Gargoyle
written and illustrated by MICHA ESTLACK

by Micha Estlack, age 17
Yukon, Oklahoma
ISBN 0-933849-63-X   Full Color

MOUSE SURPRISE
Written and illustrated by Alexandra Whitney

by Alexandra Whitney, age 8
Eugene, Oregon
ISBN 0-933849-64-8   Full Color

DON'T BUG M
written and illustrated Gillian McH

by Gillian McHale, a
Doylestown, Pennsylva
ISBN 0-933849-65-6   Full

The Incredible JELLY BEAN DAY
Written and Illustrated by TAYLOR MAW

by Taylor Maw, age 17
Visalia, California
ISBN 0-933849-66-4   Full Color

SUMMER DISCOVERY
WRITTEN AND ILLUSTRATED BY DREW CARSON

by Drew Carson, age 8
Roseburg, Oregon
ISBN 0-933849-68-0   Full Color

The Mists of Eden
NATURE'S LAST PARADISE
Written and Illustrated by Erica Sherman

by Erica Sherman, age 12
Westerville, Ohio
ISBN 0-933849-69-9   Full Color

THE PIG WENT MARCHIN OUT!
written & illustrated Justin Rigamon

by Justin Rigamonti, a
Hillsboro, Oregon
ISBN 0-933849-70-2   Full

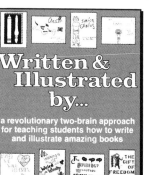

Written & Illustrated by...
a revolutionary two-brain approach for teaching students how to write and illustrate amazing books

David Melton

96 Pages • Illustrated • Softcover
ISBN 0-933849-00-1

Written & Illustrated by... by David Mel

This highly acclaimed teacher's manual offers classroom-proven, step-b
instructions in all aspects of teaching students how to write, illustrate, asse
and bind original books. Loaded with information and positive approache
really work. Contains lesson plans, more than 200 illustrations, and suggeste
tations for use at all grade levels – K through college.

The results are dazzling!
– Children's Book Review Service, Inc.

...an exceptional book!
**Just browsing through it stimulates excite-
ment for writing.**
– Joyce E. Juntune, Executive Director
American Creativity Association

A "how-to" book that really works
– Judy O'Brien, T

WRITTEN & ILLUSTRATED BY... pro
current of enthusiasm, positive th
and faith in the creative spirit of ch
David Melton has the heart of a teac
– THE READING TE